Plate 1

Bathing costume

Bathing costume

Plate 2

Golf costume

Tennis costume

Plate 3

Croquet costume

Costume for the races

Plate 4

A beau in town dress   A beau in country dress

Plate 5

Walking dress

Walking dress

Plate 6

Traveling costume

Traveling costume

Plate 7

Negligee

Nightgown

Plate 8

Visiting gown

"At home" or tea gown

Plate 9

Dinner gown

Dinner gown

Plate 10

Theater gown

Theater gown and wrap

Plate 11

Beaux-arts ball costume

Beaux-arts ball costume

Plate 12

Ball gown

Escort in tails

Plate 13

Ball gown

Escort in tails

Tom Tierney

Plate 14

Bridal gown

Groom

Plate 15

Presentation gown worn at
the English court

Plate 16